Pinkerton, Behave!

Story and pictures by

STEVEN KELLOGG

Frederick Warne

Published in Great Britain
by Frederick Warne (Publishers) Ltd, 1981
Reprinted 1981

Originally published by The Dial Press, New York, USA.
British publication rights arranged with Sheldon Fogelman

Every puppy must learn to behave. But Pinkerton just doesn't
seem to understand. In fact he gets the wrong idea entirely.
When Pinkerton is told to come, he jumps out the window.
Instead of fetching the newspaper, he chews it up. Pinkerton's
desperate owners try sending him to obedience school, but he
causes chaos and despair.
Steven Kellogg's droll story and hilarious illustrations perfectly
capture Pinkerton's many misadventures. Children are sure to
be delighted by Pinkerton, especially when he comes face to
face with a burglar and discovers a good use for his bad habits.

A Junior Literary Guild Selection in America

ISBN 0 7232 2714 4

An international co-production arranged
by Gyldendal Publishers, Copenhagen

Printed in Portugal

For Helen,
my best friend and
the person who chose
the Great Pinkerton

Every new puppy has to learn to behave.
First I'll teach Pinkerton to come when he's called.

Come!

He can learn to bring us the newspaper.

Fetch!

From now on *I'll* fetch the newspaper.

But it's important for him to defend the house if a burglar comes.

We'll pretend this dummy is a burglar.

Get the burglar, Pinkerton!

I think we need some professional help.
Pinkerton will have to go to obedience school.

When this poor creature sees how well the other dogs behave,
he will understand what we expect of him.

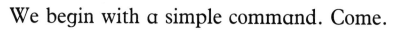

We begin with a simple command. Come.

COME! COME! COME!

COME

We cannot hold back the entire class for one confused student.
On to the next lesson!

Every dog must fetch the evening paper.

Fetch, you fleabrain, FETCH!

GRRRRRRRRRRRRRRRRRR

Our next lesson is a most important one.
Get the burglar!

Pinkerton sets a poor example for the rest of the class.
Unless he shows some improvement, he will be dismissed.

We will now review all that we have learned.
Dogs! Pay attention!

COME!

FETCH!

Mum, you and Pinkerton look pretty tired.
Why don't you go to bed and get a good night's rest?

Pleasant dreams, Pinkerton.

This is a stickup, lady. Don't move, or I'll blast you and your silly hound to chicken powder.

Pssssssst! Pinkerton! A burglar!

I warned you, lady.

GRRRRRRRRRRRrrr

Pinkerton, I'm a burglar.

I love you, Pinkerton.